SPLENDOR FROM
BROKENNESS

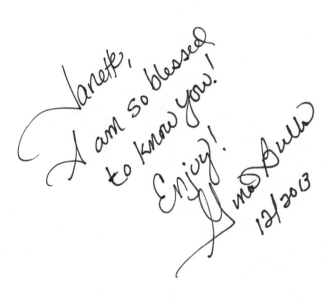

Janett,
I am so blessed
to know you!
Enjoy!
mos Brulu
12/2013

Oreta!
I am so blessed
to know you!
Enjoy!
Linda Ream
10/26/13

SPLENDOR FROM
BROKENNESS

GINA BULLIS

TATE PUBLISHING
AND ENTERPRISES, LLC

Published by Tate Publishing & Enterprises, LLC
127 E. Trade Center Terrace | Mustang, Oklahoma 73064 USA
1.888.361.9473 | www.tatepublishing.com

Tate Publishing is committed to excellence in the publishing industry. The company reflects the philosophy established by the founders, based on Psalm 68:11,
"The Lord gave the word and great was the company of those who published it."

Published in the United States of America

ISBN: 978-1-62854-413-8
1. Fiction / Christian / Romance
2. Fiction / Christian / Suspense
13.08.29

TABLE OF CONTENTS

RETURN TO DENVER

In just two short hours, Paige would be arriving in the Denver International Airport. She was looking forward to the peaceful, scenic drive to her small hometown of Mountain Home, nestled in the Rocky Mountains. She would be spending the next three weeks relaxing, skiing, and visiting a few friends.

As she leaned back in her seat, she recalled her last visit home. In one simple moment, as she closed her eyes, a mixture of memories flooded her mind and heart. Painful memories of the last time she had been home.

So much had happened during that Christmas holiday two years ago. Paige had planned a surprise visit to her parents. They were expecting her to arrive on Christmas Eve. She, however, had made plans to arrive on the 18th of December while her mom and dad were in Washington visiting her twin sister. Paige planned to spend the week baking, visiting old friends, decorating their beautiful log home, and possibly, taking in a day or two of skiing. Even with a week to do all the traditional festivities, she was not sure whether she would get to do everything she wanted to. Nonetheless, she would savor each moment.

Christmas had always been Paige's favorite time of year. Life just seemed so magical and heartwarming during the season with their traditional, twelve-foot, evergreen tree brightly decorated and fresh pine boughs and holly berries along all of the banisters. Of all the customs, her favorite Christmas tradition was setting up the beautiful, hand-carved nativity scene that her father had made. Every year, the whole family would gather around the roaring fire in the large, open room. As her father told the Christmas story, he would place each piece in its proper place on the hearth of the fireplace. To her recollection, it had always snowed on that special night. Paige decided she would wait to share this tradition with her Mom, Dad, and Brittnae.

"We are starting our final descent to the Denver International Airport" The Pilot's voice brought Paige's memories to a screeching halt. She sat forward a little dazed. Reaching up for her handbag, she pulled out her compact to freshen up. Although she was not expecting anyone to meet her at the airport, she was accustomed to maintaining a fresh, radiant appearance. It felt good to travel in comfortable clothing for a change and not her usual business attire. Paige relished the comfort and the fit of her designer jeans, wool sweater, and wool-lined leather coat. As a first-class traveler, she was one of the first off the plane.

Paige made her way through the airport to the baggage claim area. This was usually where the best-laid plans fell apart due to luggage delays—especially, when an international flight was involved. To her astonishment, her beige leather luggage pieces were among the first down the conveyor belt. Swinging two straps over her shoulder and pulling the third and heaviest piece, she turned towards the car rental counter, her last stop in the airport. As she approached, she could not help noticing a strikingly handsome, dark-haired, young man smiling her direction. As she reached the counter, he said, "Good day, Miss." Then he placed the rental form and keys on the counter.

"You must be Miss O'Conner," he said.

"How did you know my name?" Paige asked in astonishment.

"Well, your secretary gave me your flight number, arrival time and a *very good* description," he said as he winked and smiled at Paige. She felt a rush of color hit her cheeks. Then he said, "She also asked me to have your car ready the minute you arrived. So if you will allow me to take your luggage, your vehicle is waiting outside the exit to your right."

The car rental agent gently lifted the bags from Paige's shoulder and took the strap for the pull-through suitcase from her hand. Paige followed him a few feet to the door. A smile broke across her face as she noted that the SUV was her favorite color: hunter green.

"Enjoy your stay, Miss O'Connor," the agent said as he closed her door and tipped his fingers to his forehead as a departing gesture. As she pulled away from the terminal, Paige glanced at her watch. She was pleased that she had spent less than thirty minutes in the airport. *That must be some kind of record*, she thought. This trip had gone so smoothly to this point; A point of confirmation on her decision to come back. She made a mental note to pick up an extra special gift to thank her secretary Tara for the extra special details she had gone to in making her travel arrangements go so smoothly.

WINTER DRIVE

The drive to her parents' home was approximately two hours. It would be dark by the time she arrived. Traffic seemed to be extra heavy, and it was causing the stress and tension in her shoulders to mount. Paige was somewhat spoiled in London. Her condo was a quiet, three-mile drive from her boutique. On a typical daily commute, she would encounter half a dozen cars. She had forgotten the effects of heavy traffic and was relieved to see her exit off the highway. The remaining drive would be relaxing. As she turned down the two-lane road that would lead to Mountain Home, she could feel the muscles in her arms, neck, and back start to relax. Subconsciously, the heavy traffic had made her tense and stressed. The road was covered with compact snow, so she switched to four-wheel drive. As Paige gazed at the

GINA BULLIS

trees and mountains, beautifully blanketed with fresh snow, her thoughts drifted off and picked up where they had been abruptly interrupted on the plane, just prior to landing.

On the first day of her visit two years ago Paige enjoyed tromping through the snow in the crisp morning air, cutting fresh evergreen boughs. She had spent most of the afternoon rummaging through boxes of family heirlooms in the attic. She enjoyed reminiscing as she laid out each decoration, listening to Christmas music. That evening she would be having dinner with Uncle Paul and Aunt Mary. They lived just a half mile up the road. Paige was so thankful to be spending the evening with them, as well as having dinner prepared for her. She did not do much cooking and never saw the point of cooking for just one person.

Paige's step was light as she started the familiar half-mile walk to Uncle Paul and Aunt Mary's ranch. She had walked this route hundreds, if not thousands of times as she grew up. The evening was crisp and cold with a clear night sky full of stars and a beautiful moon that cast light across the snow, lighting the way. The trees were frosted from the fresh snowfall. Even with the brisk cool air, Paige felt warm inside as she walked through the snow, enjoying the night beauty of the mountains and tree line.

Before she knew it, she was at the entrance to Uncle Paul and Aunt Mary's ranch. In the distance, she could see the dim lights on what she knew was the life-size nativity scene outside their stable. Her father and uncle Paul spent several years carving each piece. It was an amazing sight, one that brought the true meaning of Christmas to life every year. Paige paused for a few moments admiring baby Jesus in the manager. "Thank you, Father, for your most precious gift," she whispered. Her thoughts were interrupted by the sound of an approaching dog. Max, her uncle Paul's faithful German shepherd of ten years, came tromping across the yard toward Paige. His pace slowed as Paige called out his name. "Hey there, Max. So I see that you are still in charge of security around here, ole boy," Paige said as she rubbed the back of his thick coat as they turned towards the house. "I bet you are looking forward to warming up by Aunt Mary's fire, just as much as I am."

There was a new pickup truck parked by the front entrance. *Wow, Uncle Paul has great taste*, she thought to herself. Aunt Mary had the door opened before Paige could ring the bell. She had her arms around Paige in a warm hearty hug before Paige could even say hello. "Oh, it is so wonderful to see you, princess. Paul and I have been so excited for your visit," Aunt Mary said with great excitement in her voice. "It is great to see you too, Aunt Mary. So is that your new toy in the driveway or Uncle Paul's? Paige asked inquisitively?

"Neither," Mary answered with a twinkle in her eye. "Why don't you warm yourself by the fire in the den. Paul is playing a game of chess with our other dinner guest."

Paige looked surprised. Her curiosity heightened. "Do I know this guest?" she asked.

"Well yes, I believe you do," Mary answered with a glimmer, somewhat mischievous look in her eyes.

Paige entered the den, finding her uncle deeply engrossed in a chess game. Paul was facing Paige's direction. She could only see the back of the other man. Paul looked up. "Paige, welcome home." As her uncle Paul moved to greet her with a hug, the other man stood to turn around. Her heart began to race. She could feel her face warming with color. Before he turned completely around, she knew by his stature that it was Garrett. As he faced Paige, his eyes smiled and his face lit up. The expression on his face clearly communicated that he was pleased with the breathtaking woman standing before him. It had been over four years since they had seen each other. Paige was even more beautiful than he remembered. Tall, slender with her dark hair cascading down her back in long, soft curls; Her face radiant with those gorgeous, green eyes that seemed to cast a spell on him whenever she looked at him. Garrett strolled towards her. "Paige, it is wonderful to see you." Reaching for her hands, he held her at arm's length. "You are stunning."

Electricity shot through her body the second he touched her hands. By now, Paige was certain that everyone in the room could hear her heart pounding in her chest. "Garrett, what a wonderful surprise!" Paige felt as though her voice was cracking. *Paige, get control of yourself.* Then as if Mary were reading her thoughts, she stepped in and said, "Dinner is ready."

Paige felt relief flood through her. She was thankful Mary had rescued her for the moment. Long ago, Paige had confided to Mary that her heart belonged to Garrett and to him alone. Their lives had gone different directions after high school, and their timing had never seemed right. As they moved to the dining room, Paige was getting the idea that, perhaps, Aunt Mary and Uncle Paul were up to something with this arranged dinner.

Conversation flowed easily during the meal. Uncle Paul was a master at filling in any gaps of silence or asking the next probing question that kept the conversation moving.

"That was another fine meal, missy," said Uncle Paul, as he winked at Aunt Mary. Missy was one of his love pet names for Mary. The sweet, tender, kindred spirit between Uncle Paul and Aunt Mary was so refreshing. You would not know they had been married for over thirty years.

"Yes, I agree. The last time I had a home-cooked meal that comes close to your cooking was the last time I dined with you and Paul," Garrett said as they all chuckled.

"Garrett and I are going to resume our chess game," Paul said. The two men stood to leave the dining room. Paige watched as they left the room.

"All right dear, Paige and I will bring the coffee and dessert in. We will be sure to save the dishes for later," Mary said with a return twinkle in her eyes. For as long as Paige could remember, her uncle Paul and aunt Mary had done dishes together.

As Paige and Mary gathered the dessert plates, coffee, and cups, Paige was about to ask Mary why she had not mentioned that Garrett would be joining them for dinner when Mary interrupted her thoughts: "Paige, dear, your Uncle Paul and I hope that we have not crossed a line of interference by inviting Garrett here this evening." Mary was facing Paige, waiting for her response. Paige smiled as she reached out and touched Mary's shoulder. "I do not know what the two of you are up to, but rest easy, you have not interfered. I am glad you invited Garrett."

"I am glad we have a few moments alone. Garrett has not taken his eyes off you since you arrived."

"Oh?" Paige answered, trying to sound as though she had not noticed even though she was keenly aware of his gaze several times during dinner.

"I don't know how you could not know. There is a lot of chemistry in the air here tonight, and I am not referring to Paul and I," Mary said with a giggle as she led the way out of the kitchen.

Mary and Paige approached the den expecting to find Paul and Garret engrossed in their attack strategies. Instead, as they came into the room, it was obvious the men were having a very serious conversation. They both stood up as the women approached. "No secrets, now," Mary said.

Garrett had been talking to Paul about Paige. It was obvious to Paul that this young man cared deeply about her, but Garrett did not realize the depth of this feelings. Paul encouraged him to spend the next several days with Paige. He knew that if they could spend time together, away from their demanding career schedules, they would have the opportunity to see the love that had been there for many years, and that was so obvious to Paul and Mary.

"Mary, that apple pie smells fantastic," Garrett said as he motioned for Paige to sit next to him. The rest of the evening was spent talking about how Garrett's business was doing. Paige was quite impressed with how successful he was. Garrett had started an international investment/consulting business right after graduate school. His company now had offices in several major cities in the United States—as well as Japan, China, and Australia. Garrett tried several times to redirect the conversation away from him, but each attempt was met with a new question from Paul. Paige enjoyed hearing what he had been doing, almost as much as she enjoyed sitting next to him. Several times during the evening, Garrett's arm or leg would brush against Paige, sending a bolt of electricity through her body. She hoped and prayed that no one noticed, even though she thoroughly enjoyed being close to him.

"Look at the time. I really should call it a night," Garrett said as he stood, and then he turned to Paige. "I noticed that you walked. May I escort you home?" There was nothing Paige wanted more. With a smile, she accepted. Garrett, always a gentleman, helped Paige with her coat. They both thanked Paul and Mary for the wonderful evening.

The moon seemed even brighter than it had been earlier that evening. The drive to Paige's parents' home was in silence, a very warm, exciting silence. As Garrett stopped the truck, he turned to Paige, gently placing his hand on her hand and said, "I am really glad that I ran into Paul today. I would not have had this time with you if I hadn't. Paige, I would really like to spend some time with you while you are home." Garrett paused before continuing. "As much time as you will allow me to." He held her in his gaze very intently. "What are your plans for tomorrow?" he asked with hopeful expectation.

Paige hesitated for a moment. She wanted to spend time with Garrett too. "Well, I was planning to decorate my folks' place. I could wait a day or two to do that. What did you have in mind?"

"No specific plans. I just want to spend the day with you. We have a lot of catching up to do. If you would like, I would love to help you decorate. I have wonderful memories of how festive their home was during the holidays. It would be great to be a part of the traditions you grew up with."

Paige's heart was swelling with excitement. "That is a wonderful idea. If you really don't mind, I would love your help. Besides, it is always more fun sharing the time with someone special." Once again, Paige felt certain Garrett could hear her heart pounding in her chest.

"It is settled then. What time should your helper arrive?" Garrett asked with his spellbinding smile.

"Let's get started at eight. I will fix you breakfast," Paige answered, somewhat bewildered at her statement regarding breakfast, as she had not cooked in a long time.

"Eight is fine," Garrett said as he got out of the truck. Paige was moved just watching him walk toward her. He walked her to the door. At the door, she was aware of how close he was standing to her. As he looked into her eyes, he said, "I cannot remember when I have enjoyed myself like I have tonight." With that, he bent down and gently kissed her on the cheek. "I will see you in the morning, sunshine." He had not called her that since high school. He had bestowed that name on her because he said no matter what life threw his way—Paige brought sunshine to his day. If asked to identify all the emotions that were rushing through her heart, soul, mind, and body at that moment, Paige would have been speechless. From inside, she watched Garrett drive away. She had such warmth in her heart that she had not noticed how chilly it was in the great room. She turned to the fireplace and saw there were still coals. She stoked the fire, grabbed her favorite wool blanket, and curled up on the couch to recount the events of the evening. Gazing at the flames, she drifted off to sleep.

UNEXPECTED PLANS

Paige awoke a little bewildered: *Why am I on the couch?* She had slept so soundly she was somewhat disoriented. She tried to recall what she was doing or thinking about at the time she must have drifted off to sleep. The last thing she remembered was thinking about Garrett and how their friendship had grown all through high school and college. Paige had always felt something very special for Garrett. Their connection was deeper than any other relationship she knew, even with her twin sister. They had a soul connection. She had never told him how she felt. In fact, her sister Brittnae and Aunt Mary were the only two people she had ever shared that secret with. In high school, Paige had spent a lot of time with Garrett. They were inseparable; skiing, horseback riding, running, playing tennis. Although college sent them in different directions, they always kept in touch. Paige had always hoped their friendship would develop into a deeper relationship, but it seemed as though they were both very intent on their individual goals and careers. Neither one made time for a serious relationship with someone else. The fact that Garrett was so "married" to his career made Paige believe there was still hope for them. They were both very stable, successful business owners. Perhaps, the timing was now. The mantle clock chime, marking half past the hour, brought Paige back to the present. She glanced at the clock, and a rush of panic hit her. It was seven thirty. She had wanted to take a little, extra time to get ready before Garrett arrived. She would have to settle for a quick shower, light makeup, comfy jeans, and a sweater. She was just putting on her jewel, green sweater when she heard Garrett at the front door. She lightly misted herself with her favorite perfume before opening the door.

"Good morning." Garrett's greeting was electrifying.

"Good morning," Paige responded. As she led him towards the kitchen, Garrett said, "Something smells yummy." Paige turned around to say "I have not started cooking yet…" when she caught his approving eye—she knew he was referring to her.

She quickly turned around, hoping he had not noticed the flush of color to her face.

Garrett was handy in the kitchen. "Are you interested in one of my famous omelets?" Garrett asked.

"I thought I was cooking breakfast for you; but I am certainly game for one of your omelets," Paige answered with a sparkle in her eyes.

Breakfast was a huge success. The best part was the company. It was just like old times, except this time—Paige constantly had to keep her heart in check. She was certain of her feelings for Garrett. They had been there for the past ten years. When they were thousands of miles apart, it was much easier to keep her feelings hidden deep in her heart. Being with Garrett was going to present a challenge. She was more than ready to bring them above the surface. She deeply loved him but was not certain of how deep his feelings for her were. She knew that she could be hurt if she was not careful. So far, Garrett had been very sweet and charming but had not given her any indication that his feelings for her were more than they had been in the past. He had always been a little flirtatious, affectionate, charming, and somewhat generous with his attention. She was determined to enjoy his company—with a guarded heart.

"I could sit here all day talking with you, Paige. We have always been able to talk for hours. But I believe we have some Christmas decorating to do. So what do you say, shall we get started?" Garrett stood as he spoke. Paige was surprised at how much she liked him taking charge. She was so accustomed to being the one in charge. While growing up, she was the one to make things happen or motivate Brittnae. As a thriving business owner, she was in the captain's seat.

"Yes, let's get started," she said.

They spent the rest of the morning moving boxes of Christmas heirlooms and treasures from the attic to the great room—the center of Christmas in the O'Connor home. The day seemed to fly by. At six in the evening, they both collapsed on the couch in front of the fireplace. "Woman, you really know how to work a guy. I may think twice before volunteering for the next project," Garret chided, flashing a very flirtatious smile.

"I am amazed at how much we have accomplished in one day. This project usually takes my family at least two days." Paige's voice was a mixture of astonishment and excitement, as she knew she now had the next few days free.

Garrett smiled. "Does this mean your schedule is clear for the next few days?" he asked with excitement in his voice.

"Well, yes. Actually, I had set aside the last two days of the week for a 'cushion' for visiting."

"Great," Garrett interrupted Paige. "That means I can have you all to myself for the next four days."

Garrett's tone was part asking, part assuming he had her to himself. Paige was not sure how to read him. Without a moment's hesitation, she answered, "I am free. What do you have planned for us?"

Garrett rattled off a list of ideas including skiing, sledding, Christmas shopping, ice-skating, long walks. "You name it, and we will do it." Garrett walked over to Paige and took both of her hands in his. "What I want is to spend time with you. I have missed you more than you know." Garrett's words seemed so genuine. Paige wanted desperately to know how he felt about her. She was determined not to rush him. She would enjoy his company, and maybe, by the end of the week, she would know.

ANTICIPATION

The days with Garrett flew by. They seemed like only hours. Their time was filled with laughter, fun activities, hours of talking, and numerous, subtle hints of deep feelings. Paige had never enjoyed herself more than she had during the time spent with Garrett. He had been a perfect gentleman. Her favorite times were the evenings when they would sit by the fire and talk for hours. The evenings together were romantic, at least from Paige's point of view. On their last evening together before her parents were to return, Paige still did not have a hunded percent confirmation of how Garrett felt. She was certain that he cared for her. How deep it was—was the mystery. His eyes seemed to tell Paige how he felt. When he looked into her eyes, it was as if he reached down to touch her soul. There was absolutely no way to express how his gaze affected her. She knew they would talk tonight. If he did not open the opportunity, she would ask. She had to know where they stood before returning to London. She did not—could not return without knowing how he felt.

"I have some 'business' details to attend to this afternoon," Garret said. "I will pick you up at six for dinner. Be sure to dress warm," he said in a somewhat conspiring tone. Garrett had a very special evening planned and needed the afternoon to take care of the details.

"What are you up to?" Paige asked.

"Hey, young lady, Christmas is no time for questions. We have had four incredible days together, and I am giving you the afternoon off from time with me." He kissed her sweetly on the cheek and walked out the door. The smell of her skin and hair had an intoxicating effect on him. He took a deep breath of fresh air as he walked to his truck. Adrenaline and emotions like a raging river flowed through his body. He pulled out his list of to-dos as he drove toward town.

Paige spent the afternoon wrapping Christmas gifts and listening to her favorite Christmas songs. She even had time for a quick nap before getting ready. She took extra time curling her hair. Pulling her hair back with full, soft curls was Garrett's favorite.

DATE GONE WRONG

Garrett arrived promptly at six in the evening. He had planned every intricate detail of this evening. He wanted so desperately to make Paige happy. Filled with anticipation and excitement for the evening, he bolted up the front steps. When Paige opened the door, he was overwhelmed with her beauty. It was hard to comprehend how she could appear more beautiful with each encounter. Paige wore a beautiful wool coat, covering a jewel-colored cashmere sweater and black pants, which according to Garrett, fit very nice. "You are stunning," Garrett said as he held out his hand to take hers. He paused for a few moments to "drink" her in. As he bent to lightly kiss her cheek, he whispered, "Close your eyes, I have a surprise for you."

Paige's heart was racing with excitement. She took his hand, and he led her around the corner of the house where he had parked the sleigh. "Okay, open your eyes," Garrett said. "A horse-drawn sleigh." Paige gasped with almost a school girl's excitement. "Your chariot awaits, your majesty," Garrett said as he helped her into the sleigh.

Paige watched him as he walked in front of the horses and climbed into the sleigh next to her. He was so handsome, and when he walked, he carried himself in such a way that exuded strength, confidence, and security.

It was a perfect night for a sleigh ride: clear sky filled with stars and a half moon. Garrett directed the horses through the woods toward a small cabin—a popular rest stop for snowmobilers and cross-country skiers to warm up. The wind seemed to cut through Paige's coat. She started to shiver. Feeling her body quiver, Garrett put his arm around her and drew her even closer to him. "I don't know why you were sitting so far away in the first place," Garrett said, nuzzling his face in Paige's hair. Paige felt as if her body had been electrically shocked. No one made her feel the way he did. She melted against him for the rest of the ride. Garrett felt a rush through his body as he held Paige. He had finally come to the realization of how much he loved and needed her. He did not want to live without her any longer. Tonight was the night he planned to tell her.

As the sleigh drew closer to the cabin, Paige noticed a soft light inside. "There must be some night snowmobilers out," she said with disappointment in her voice. Garrett smiled to himself but did not say a word.

Garrett stopped the sleigh and jumped to the ground. He held out his hand for Paige. She jumped down. As she landed, she realized that she was in the arms of the man she loved, looking into his face. Garrett was smiling down at her. It took every ounce of his strength to not hold her, kiss her, and tell her how he felt right then. No, he had planned everything, and this was not the moment to tell her. "Let's go inside," he said, and as he opened the door, Paige stopped in the doorway. There in front of her was a beautiful table set for two. A vase of roses stood between the two white candles that lit the room. There was a crackling fire in the fireplace and soft music playing. Paige could not believe her eyes. Turning to Garrett, she said, "This is the most romantic, beautiful setting I have ever seen." Her voice was full of emotion. Garrett was moved by her reaction. He wanted so badly to make her happy. Up until now, he had been unsure of the depth of Paige's feelings for him. There were times when he saw some clues, but then, she would pull herself back. It was as if she would start to open the door to her heart, but something was guarding her from opening her heart completely. But now, as she stood looking deep into his eyes, he was sure she was ready to give him her heart. Looking into her eyes, it was if he could see her soul. Her eyes communicated her love deeper and louder than any verbal message. He pulled her to him. "I am so glad you like it" he said in a whisper. Garrett pulled back far enough to look into her eyes. "I love you, Paige. I can't believe that it has taken me so many years to realize what you mean to me. But I know without a doubt or reservation that I love you with all my heart, and I want to spend the rest of my life with you by my side."

Paige could barely breathe. She had waited and wanted this moment for so long. He tenderly lifted her chin, lowering his lips to meet hers. Paige melted in his embrace and answered his kiss with all the yearning she had kept inside of her. He tenderly kissed her check, neck, and lips, while repeatedly saying "I love you."

"I love you too, Garrett. I have loved you for so long and have wanted to tell you." She loved being in his arms. His strong body provided protection and safety she longed for.

The evening was like a fairy tale. Dancing, talking of their future, lost in each other's gaze. They both were thinking this would be the best Christmas of their lives. Neither one knew that their newly claimed happiness was about to be shattered.

Paige and Garrett were just sitting down to the table when they heard snowmobiles approaching the cabin. "I will go check it out, you sit tight," Garrett said. Paige chuckled at the thought of her romantic dinner with Garrett being interrupted to include some cold snowmobilers. That would be a fun memory. She was still smiling to herself when Garrett returned. He stopped in the doorway—his face was an ashen grey. He looked like he was in shock. "Garrett, what is the matter?" Paige asked with panic in her voice. Garrett did not answer. He walked across the room and wrapped his arms around Paige and held her tightly. He just stroked her hair and held her tight. He could not get any sound out. His body was shaking. Paige pulled herself away. She looked past him. Garrett had left the door to the cabin open. Paige had a clear view of the snowmobilers. They were police officers. She looked back at Garrett. "Garrett, what is it? You are scaring me. What's happened?" she asked, the panic and fear had escalated in her voice.

Looking into her eyes, he said, "Paige, there has been an accident. Your mom, dad, and Brittnae were involved."

"Are they ok? What hospital are they...." Garrett interrupted Paige, taking her in his arms again and held her. With a quaking in his voice and his body shaking, he said, "They are gone, baby. There were no survivors."

"No! No! There has to be a mistake." Paige slumped to a chair shaking her head no. She kept saying they were wrong, and that it was someone else's family. Garrett motioned for the police to come in.

Through tear-filled eyes, Paige recognized the two officers: Officer Gage, one of her dad's closest friends and Officer Stewart, one of her and Garrett's classmates. Officer Gage knelt beside Paige. In a voice full of compassion, he said, "Paige, I am so sorry, sweet heart, this is one of the toughest messages I have ever had to deliver. When I heard the emergency call, I requested to be the person to talk with you. Your dad was like a brother to me. We do have a positive identification on all three victims." Officer Gage sat silently with Paige for a few minutes.

Paige overheard Garrett talking with Officer Stewart, asking if they knew any details of the accident. The only details they knew at this point was that it was a single car accident. The conditions were icy, and the driver lost control of the car. There were no survivors when the rescue unit arrived. Garrett could not take his eyes off of Paige while the officer was explaining the details. He felt as if someone was ripping his heart into two. He was not sure he could bear watching the woman he loved bear such a load of pain.

The rest of the night was a blur to Paige. She could not recall the ride back to the house. Paul and Mary had been there to offer support. Garret refused to leave Paige alone. He held her in his arms through the night. He would do everything in his power to help her through this dark valley of sadness and loss. It had taken him several years to realize what she meant to him and how much he loved and needed her. Garrett cried out to God, "How could a night that started out with such promise and hope end in despair and sadness? Only you, Lord, will sustain both of us through this. Comfort Paige. Help me be the man she needs. Only you can comfort us and carry us through this dark hour. Amen."

Garrett had planned to ask Paige to marry him back at the cabin. Now, he knew that he would need to wait. Paige was going to need time to heal from this horrific loss. It did not matter how long, he would wait for her.

AN UNEXPECTED
FUNERAL GUEST

Paige awoke the morning of the funeral. Everything took such effort. Showering, dressing, she seemed to have no energy. She was lacing up her boots when she heard footsteps from the porch. It would be Garrett. He had slept on the couch every night to be close to Paige. Paige had wanted to be alone last night. Much against his wishes, Garrett honored her request. She glanced at the clock. Garrett was early. She was relieved to know that she would have his strength to lean on to get through the day. She opened the door and welcomed Garrett's embrace. They walked to his truck in silence. As he opened her door, Garrett paused and turned Paige toward him. He lifted her chin so he could look into her eyes. "I love you, Paige. We will get through this day and the days to come." He gently kissed her.

As they drove to Paul and Mary's, Paige knew she would not have made it through the past few days if it had not been for Garrett, Paul, and Mary. Paul and Mary oversaw the funeral arrangements. They knew Paige would have enough decisions to make. She had decided to postpone the funeral until Thursday, two days after Christmas. Paige was moved by the support from the community who came to pay last respects to her parents and Brittnae. The service was simple and brief, just as they would have wanted. Paige was the last to leave the grave site. Garrett was standing a few feet from her. Kneeling beside the caskets, in tears, she said, "Good bye, Mum and Pop. I miss you terribly. Sis, there will always be a void in my heart that only a sister can fill." She remained kneeling for several minutes.

Paige stood and turned to Garrett. Her eyes met his momentarily before quickly moving past him to a man approximately twenty yards behind him. "Sam?" she gasped in disbelief. Sam had been a foster child with the O'Connor family during her junior high and high school years. After high school, Sam traveled to Europe. Other than an occasional phone call, he all but disappeared from the O'Connors' lives.

Sam started walking towards her and Garrett. As Sam closed the distance between them, Garrett pulled Paige close to his side. He sensed her uneasiness. With tears in his eyes, Sam said, "Paige, I can't believe this. I can't believe they are gone."

Paige was irritated at his pretense. He had always been very good at drama and a false front. "How did you know?" Paige asked. "Paul and Mary have been trying to contact you but were not able to locate you."

"I have been traveling the past few weeks. Stopping here for the holidays has been part of my travel plans. It has been several years since I have been back and thought the holidays were a perfect time to make a surprise visit. I just arrived in town late yesterday and heard the news."

It was starting to get dark, and the wind had picked up. "Paige," Garrett said, "we should go over to Paul and Mary's." Paige was grateful that he redirected the conversation.

"Oh Sam, you remember Garrett Storm?" Paige asked.

"Yeah, nice to see you again," Sam said, reaching out to shake Garrett's hand. Garrett returned the gesture then returned his arm to Paige's waist. Paige snuggled close to him as they walked towards the house. She felt a chill deep inside. A chill not tied to the weather but rather to Sam's presence.

Mary met them at the door. "Paige, you must be chilled to…." Mary stopped abruptly as she recognized the man standing behind Paige on the porch. "Sam?" she asked with a mixture of surprise and shock in her voice.

Her eyes moving back to make contact with Paige. Garrett interrupted, "Mary, I am going to take Paige in the library to warm by the fire." He and Paige left Mary and Sam to reconvene their greeting.

Settled on a comfortable couch by the roaring fire, Paige let herself drift away. The music and the light chatter had a balming effect on her aching heart and soul. She was lost in the warmth of the crackling fire when Garrett returned with a hot drink and a plate of food. "You have not eaten a good meal in days," he said as he sat down next to her and handed her the plate. Paige was so grateful for Garrett. She loved how he was so in tune to her needs.

"I would like nothing more than to sit with you, however, Paul needs some assistance outside. A few guests are leaving, and their cars are stuck in the snow."

"Hurry back. I really need you to be with me." Paige's attention went back to the fire. She had a few bites of food before drifting off to sleep.

She woke to a man's hand on her shoulder. It was Sam. He was sitting next to her on the couch. "We have a lot to catch up on, sis." Paige had always been uncomfortable with him calling her that. She was not his sister. They had never been close. If things had been different when he lived with them, then possibly, their relationship would be more like siblings. Paige's father had been named Sam's legal guardian before his parents had died in a plane crash. Sam had moved in with them when he was thirteen. He left the day after graduation, and the years between were years she would rather not relive. Sam had an attitude that the world owed him. This often came out as though Paige's parents owed him.

"Well, sis, you will be sitting really pretty after the estate is settled."

Paige was appalled at what she was hearing. His words stung like the bitter cold. She glared at him in disbelief. She stood up, spilling her plate of food. "Excuse me, I have nothing to say to you." Paige quickly made her way to the kitchen hoping to find Mary.

She was not there, but Sam was, quick at her heels. "Hey, sis, why are you running from me? This is not a very warm welcome for your brother." Sam reached out to grab Paige's arm, turning her to face him. His grip on her arm was painfully tight, and he pulled her close to his body. Paige could smell alcohol on his breath, and the look in his eyes was unnerving.

"What do you say we go back to our house and talk?" he said with a look in his eyes that sent an arctic chill through Paige's veins. "Our house!" she said, barely able to get the words out. "What do you mean our house?" Paige's voice was filled with a mixture of emotions loud enough to be heard by guests. Through the door across the room, Garrett entered the kitchen. He had overheard Paige's voice. In two long strides, he was at Paige's side, wedging his body between Paige and Sam. The look in his eyes, the tone of his voice, and his presence were powerful and intimidating. Sam released his grip on Paige and took a few steps back. "What's your problem, Mr. Storm? A little protective, are we?" His voice was filled with sarcasm.

"Sam, you won't be accompanying Paige anywhere," Garrett said in a stern voice. The look in his eyes matched his tone as he closed the space between him and Paige. "Paul and Mary have reserved a room for you at the Best Western in town."

Sam glanced at Paige as he reluctantly accepted the offer. As he left the kitchen to rejoin the other guests in the library, he glanced over his shoulder with a final parting message: "We will have plenty of opportunity to catch up, sis."

Garrett moved Paige toward the back door. "Good night, Mary, Paul. Thank you for all you have done today. We will stop by tomorrow." Paige hugged Paul and Mary before stepping outside into the cold, brisk, winter air.

The rest of the night was a blur to Paige. She did not remember the ride back to the house. Garrett refused to leave Paige alone, especially after the encounter with Sam. He held her in his arms through the night.

Paige lived in a state of shock over the next several days. Garrett had been a tremendous help in taking care of final matters. She was so grateful to have his expertise in settling the financial matters, especially with the added stress that Sam's presence brought. She trusted Garrett, implicitly. Her parents had invested wisely. The one decision Paige was not willing to make was to keep or sell their home. That decision would have to wait until a future date. With the funeral behind her and the financial matters nearly settled, she yearned to return to London. Sitting around here only heightened her pain and sadness. She had to return to work, her haven, her shelter from dealing with the pain.

Paige characteristically retreated to self-preservation and hiding when pain was heavy. Not the ideal way of dealing with pain. But survival was her first step. She knew in time she would have to courageously face her heart and walk toward and through her pain. The time was not now. The pain was too great, too intense. She was not ready to walk through that valley.

She had been away for four weeks and was certain that burying herself in her work would lessen the pain and help her get on with her life. She also wanted to put an ocean between her and Sam. His presence stirred ice in her veins that she had long forgotten, or at least *thought* she had forgotten.

LONDON

It was a beautiful, sunny morning. Paige heard a vehicle outside, approaching the house. That would be Garrett. He had left early this morning to help Paul with a load of firewood. Paige was a little surprised that he was returning so early. Paige had grown accustomed to starting her day with him.

How is he going to take my news of returning to London? The doorbell brought her thoughts to a halt. As she approached the door, she was suddenly overcome with an unnerving feeling. She paused momentarily then opened the door. "Good morning, Paige," Sam said in an eerie tone. She started to close the door when Sam pushed by her. "Not a warm welcome. What is it with you? You are so cold and uncaring towards me. We used to be so close. You have been avoiding me like the plague." His tone and the way he was looking at Paige made her very uncomfortable.

Paige knew she would not be able to convince him to wait in his car until Garrett arrived. He made her feel nervous and intimidated. Paige walked towards the couch and sat down in the chair next to the couch where Sam was sitting. Taking a deep breath to relax, she asked, "Sam, why are you here?"

"I think you know why I am here. It has been two weeks since the funeral. I know you have had Mr. Storm finalized the financial matters. I want to know how much your parents left to me. Perhaps they left me the house."

Sam's tone was chilling and desperate. Paige stared at Sam in disbelief. She hated that he made her feel afraid. She wanted desperately to grab him, slap, and shake him and yell "You are *not* in the will, get out of my life once and for all! After what you did to Brittnae in high school, do you really think my parents would leave you a dime? You are lucky that you are not locked up somewhere." She was about to answer him when there were loud footsteps at the door, and then the door burst open. Garrett's stance all but filled the doorway.

"Your knight has arrived to save you," Sam hissed in a low tone.

"What the hell are you doing here?" Garrett demanded as he stormed across the room and grabbed Sam. Garrett's

6'5" stature towered over Sam's 5'11". With his anger and ingrained drive to protect, this was an intimidating scene.

"I came by to see Paige before she left for London," Sam answered glancing at Paige, giving her a wink of victory.

How could he know? she thought to herself. She had not even told Mary and Paul yet. She had wanted to talk with Garrett first. She was enraged that he would drop this bomb on Garrett. Paige turned to Garrett. His face communicated a mixture of emotions: anger, confusion, surprise. "Garrett, I was planning to tell you this morning. This was not the way I had intended you to find out I am leaving. I have no idea how Sam knows."

"We'll talk about this later. For now, Mr. Peterson will be leaving." Garrett escorted Sam to the door. Stopping a few feet before the opening, he bent towards Sam and spoke. His words were too quiet for Paige to hear, but from the expression on Sam's face, Paige knew that Sam conceded and knew that Garrett meant what he said. Sam stepped back and moved towards the door. As he turned the doorknob, he turned and said, "You have not seen the last of Sam Peterson. Paige, I will be back to collect what is mine." He paused as he looked her over from head to toe. "Everything that is mine." He slammed the door. Sam's parting words made her sick to her stomach. Memories from the horrific night ten years ago when he attacked Brittnae flooded her mind.

Paige was enraged, scared, and exhausted. In two week's time, she went from what seemed like a mountain top to the pits of hell, emotionally. She slumped to the couch and buried her face in her hands. She was so tired of crying. Garrett sat next to her and took her in his arms, as he had so many times the past several weeks. Garrett was not prepared to be apart from her. He knew that Paige would be doing herself more harm by ignoring the pain and burring herself into a work rut. He knew from experience. That was what he had done when he lost his parents. They had not talked about their future since the night of the accident. Garret had not wanted to rush her or push her away, but he had not planned on her leaving.

As her body relaxed in his arms, he lifted her tear-streaked face and asked. "Why?" It was the only word he could choke out. His eyes filled with tears as he searched her eyes. Those spellbinding eyes that held his soul a few days earlier that communicated a love deeper than he could imagine were now clouded with pain and fear. He felt powerless.

"I have to get on with my life," she said. "I cannot stay around here any longer. The pain is too fresh, and I have the added daily fears of Sam's presence."

Paige said as she looked into Garrett's eyes. His eyes were filled with a mixture of longing and fear. Fear of being apart from her. Paige sat up and took his hands in hers. "The last thing I want to do is hurt you. I love you with all my heart. I need you more than I have ever needed anyone. But I need to find myself and heal. This house is full of memories. There is too much pain here. The past few weeks, the overwhelming emotions I have felt of love, sadness, loss, suspicion, and fear. That part of my heart needs to heal so that I can love you freely. I need finality to my parent's and Brittnae's deaths."

Tears filled his eyes as he gently squeezed her hands. Looking into her eyes, it was as though all the life had drained out of her. The vigor, the spunk, the lively part of Paige was missing. He whispered, "I love you, Paige. I love you more than I believed possible to love another person. I cannot see my life without you. I know that you need time to heal, I just don't agree with you burying yourself and hiding. I know from experience that is not the best way to deal with grief."

Paige was angered by his words. "Who are you to tell me how to grieve? I have lost my entire family." She moved away from Garrett. With determination and resolve in her voice, she said, "I can't sleep. I can't think clearly. Right now, I need to be where things make sense, and that is London."

There was a long period of silence before Garrett responded. He knew that she was exhausted, and he was trying with every ounce of his energy and the tremendous grace God was providing, to put her needs first. "I know your company needs you, and I respect that. I want you to know how much I need you too. You say you want to get on with your life. Where do *we* fit into that picture? If you cannot answer me now, I will wait." He lifted her chin, looking into her eyes, he said, "I will support whatever decision you make and give you as much time as you need. You have my heart. This Christmas has dealt you a severe blow, but please remember that it was this Christmas that we realized the depth of our love. You have another family waiting… us." With that final word, Garrett took Paige's face in his hands and kissed her tenderly.

DRIVE OF SILENCE

The drive to the airport was silent, but it was a comfortable silence. Just being away from the house lifted weight from Paige's shoulders.

Nestled close to Garrett, she felt safe. Paige was so exhausted she slept the whole drive. Garrett pulled up to the rental car area. He put his arm around Paige and whispered, "Paige, we are here." They worked their way to a restaurant near her gate. They had two hours before her flight. Paige had been thinking about yesterday's encounter between Sam and Garrett. "What did you say to Sam yesterday?" Garrett hesitated before answering. "You do not have to worry yourself about Sam. I will take care of him. He knows I mean business. I saw it in his eyes." Paige wanted to press Garrett to be more specific but reconsidered, since they did not have much time together. She did not want their last hour together to be strained.

"We had better go," he said. "Your plane will be boarding soon."

As they walked toward the security clearance, the point of separation, Garret held so tightly to Paige's hand that it hurt. Paige started to say something when Garrett stopped, turned her towards him and held her in his arms. He buried his face in her hair and whispered, "I love you. I love you so much. I need you, and I am praying that you come back to me soon." Paige felt his tears on her cheek and neck. He lifted her chin and covered her mouth with his. The passion and love he poured out consumed her. Pulling away was the hardest thing she ever had to do. She pulled away and smiled. "I love you, always and forever. I will be back soon." She turned toward her plane.

Garrett's heart ached as he watched her go. How long would it be until she was back in his arms to stay? He turned to check in for his return flight to New York. The irony was that he would be burying himself in his work, and more importantly, the investigation of the accident.

FLIGHT TO NEW YORK

G arrett's flight back to New York was filled with a mixture of deep emotions for Paige, as well as the investigation of the accident that killed Paige's family. He suspected that Sam was, somehow, involved in this accident, but he had to prove it. Sam had been involved in numerous shady operations. Resolution to this unsolved accident was the key to Paige's healing.

From the airport, Garrett drove directly to his office. He did not want to waste anytime toward getting started. The silence was broken by a call from his secretary: "Mr. Storm, Paul Stevens is on line two for you. He says it is urgent."

"Good morning, Paul."

"Good morning, Garrett." Paul's voice was filled with intensity. "Garrett, I have some leads on Sam. He has several issues. Unfortunately, I do not have the connections to see how deep and far these issues go. I am hoping that you have the connections, both nationally and internationally to retrieve the information we need to pull this puzzle together. From the information I was able to pull from records, he has drug connections and owes several hundred thousand to unnoted organizations."

"Thank you, Paul. I am confident that my national and international contacts will be able to help fill in the gaps."

"Garrett, there is one more thing. Mary had an unnerving conversation with Sam yesterday. He stated that his business was sending him to London for the next several months. We are concerned that he may stalk Paige."

After brief silence on the phone, Garrett responded, "Thank you. I am going to take care of that right now. We will be in touch. Good-bye, Paul."

Garrett hung up the phone and immediately contacted a colleague in the detective field in London: "John, Garrett here. I am hoping that you are available to cover a personal request. I need 24/7 surveillance/protection for Paige O'Connor. She is the owner of O'Conner Architectural Design in Sevenoaks, London. I will forward a classified packet of information to you related to the individual who may be attempting to contact her. I will be in contact with Ms. O'Connor to let her know what is going on."

LANGSHOTT MANOR

A few weeks after returning to London, one of Paige's major clients, Erika VanHieden, stopped in to offer her condolences. Erika was from a very wealthy family and Paige's firm had worked on numerous designs for several VanHieden properties. The VanHiedens, a prominent family, were not discreet about flaunting their wealth. Erika was instrumental in ensuring that O'Conner design was published in several high end London magazines. Paige was extremely proud of her work, as some of her most creative design work was done for the VanHieden family.

"Paige, are you available to meet me for brunch on Sunday in Gatwick. It will give us a chance to visit and catch up." Erika was planning to discuss a contract opportunity with Paige. The VanHieden family had recently acquired a historic property. The manor is in need of extensive refurbishing, design and décor. Paige's style was exactly what Erika was looking for.

Paige agreed to meet with Erika that following Sunday. Throughout the week, time passed excruciatingly slow. Her client project board had limited work. Paige had completed the majority of projects prior to leaving for her holiday trip in Colorado. Her plan at the time was to have a light project load when she returned from the holidays so she could ease her way back into the daily work; a great idea at the time, as she anticipated that she would be returning from a fun, relaxing, memory filled trip. On the contrary, returning from a grief filled trip, Paige wanted a packed schedule; one that required her to work 14-16 hours a day. Her methods, although not the healthiest, were Paige's method for working through stress, grief, tragedy. "If I work hard, long hours; sleep comes easier with exhaustion; no time to "feel". Two weeks had passed since her return and she had yet to land any new contracts.

Sunday finally arrived. It was a beautiful day. Paige enjoyed the thirty minute drive in the country to the small restaurant to meet Erika. Paige forgot how refreshing a drive through the country side could be. As she walked to the door of the restaurant, her stride was noticeably light. "Thank you, Lord for this beautiful day. Thank you for your mercies that are new every morning"

"Good morning, Erika." Erika was pleased to see that Paige' spirits were light and enthusiastic.

"Good morning, Paige." Erika rose from her chair and gave Paige a hug. For the next half hour conversation was light and easy. Erika was a natural at navigating conversations. She steered the conversation from light, easy topics towards her agenda item. "Paige, I had a conversation with Tara before you returned from Colorado. She indicated that your project board was light. I don't know if you are aware that my family has acquired the Langshott Manor property, right here in Gatwick. The manor is in need of your magic. I would love to tour the property with you today and discuss the possibility of O'Conner Architectural Design providing the design, refurbishing and décor. Erika paused, giving Paige time to process her pitch.

Paige was intrigued by Erika's idea. "You are correct; my current project load is light. This is a great time to consider a large project. My day is open. Let's tour the property and discuss the scope of work.

Over the next four hours Erika guided Paige through fifteen thousand square feet of historic structure. The plan was to refurbish the facility, preserving the historic architecture; the facility would be marketed as an excellent vacation stay, as well as a five star location for special events; corporate conferences, weddings, family reunions, etc.

Throughout the tour, Paige's mind raced with ideas. She felt a renewed energy and excitement that she had not had since that horrific night at the cabin. This project would be the perfect escape for her to immerse herself into; therapy to help her cope with the nagging grief of losing her family. Beyond that, this project would take her architectural design business to an entirely new level.

"Paige," Erika interrupted Paige's thoughts, " I am prepared to offer you a contract for the work. O'Conner work, hands down, is the unanimous choice by the entire VanHieden family." Paige was greatly moved by the compliment.

Erika continued, "I would like to schedule a time to meet with you this week to discuss contract terms and get the project underway. What day works best for you?" Paige pulled up her calendar on her iphone. "How does Monday at 10:00 a.m. sound?"

"Perfect. You can pull up a full array of pictures of the property on our website." Erika extended her hand to Paige; shaking her hand, she said, "Paige, I look forward to partnering with you on yet another VanHieden project."

Monday morning at the office, Tara was surprised to see Paige in the office when she arrived. Coffee made, computers turned on. Typically, Tara arrived at least 30 minutes before Paige, especially on a Monday morning. "Good morning, Paige. How was your weekend?"

"Good morning, Tara. My weekend was excellent." Paige's response was full of enthusiasm. "Wow, you have quite the twinkle in your eye. What are you up to?

Did Garrett make a surprise visit this weekend?" Tara asked inquisitively.

"No, but I have some amazing news. Our project board is about to transform from light to full. We have a meeting with Erika VanHieden this morning at 10:00 to discuss the terms of a new contract, for what I consider an opportunity of a lifetime. The VanHieden family has acquired the Langshott Manor and they want to contract with O'Conner Architectural Design to design and refurbish the manor."

"That is so exciting. That large of a project is going to keep us extremely busy. Have you shared the news with Garrett?"

"I am planning to call him once we have the contract details confirmed. I will be in my office drafting a contract. Please let me know when Erika arrives."

The meeting with Erika was smooth and concluded with the most lucrative contract O'Conner Architectural Design had ever had. Paige would need to work exclusively with Erika over the next 10-12 months. She was eager to get the project off the ground.

Paige welcomed the busy schedule. It distracted her from her grief, as well as the pending investigation of Sam and his involvement in the accident.

For the next several weeks Paige was so engaged in the redesign work that she noticed she was sleeping better at night, and really felt as though she was beginning to work through the grief. The project involved several meetings every week, as well as traveling to research and view design and décor ideas. Erika accompanied Paige on several of the trips. Paige found that they had a lot in common. She also enjoyed conversing with Erika on non-work related topics. Erika was becoming a friend and confidant to Paige.

Approximately midway through the project, Paige began thinking about making a return trip to Colorado. She knew that she had unfinished business to attend to. She also desperately wanted to reopen her heart to Garrett. She had basically shut down after her parents and Brittane died. The pain was unbearable. How does one process extreme grief and soul- deep love at the same time? Paige was not capable of navigating the sea of extreme emotions. She chose her safe survival mode – dive deep into work and deal with her grief. She wanted to be whole and full of life and love, not burdened with grief, when she returned to Garrett.

Garrett and Paige shared the common approach to dealing with extreme pain. He too had returned to his work and buried himself into insane hours. Paige was unaware that his schedule also included an extensive investigation of Sam.

On a recent visit to the Langshott Manor to preview construction updates, Paige shared with Erika, her plans to travel to Colorado the following December. Erika's reaction was slightly odd. Paige thought perhaps Erika was concerned that the project would not be complete by the holiday. Erika's response was based on an entirely different set of reasons, unknown to Paige.

"Erika, the project is ahead of schedule by several weeks. I do not anticipate any delays. We have all the fabric, décor materials on order. I am confident this project will be complete in late October. The early completion will allow for the booking of holiday events." Paige was seeking to reassure Erika that her trip to Colorado would be well after the completion of the project. Erika's initial response of concern quickly turned to acceptance of Paige's comments. "You are right, I over reacted." With that exchange, Erika quickly transitioned the conversation towards Paige's trip. "So, do you have your travel details? Will Garrett be joining you?"

"I have not made any travel arrangements at this time. I will most likely wait until August or September before finalizing the details. For now, I am planning to keep my plans to myself, as I want to surprise Garrett. He is planning to spend the holidays with my Uncle Paul and Aunt Mary."

INVESTIGATION

All afternoon, Paige was consumed with her meeting with Erika. To her surprise, the afternoon drifted by quickly. She closed her shop for the day. As she closed the shop door, she noticed a man across the street looking at her. A chill went up her spine. She wished that she had arranged for Tara to give her a ride home. Paige's car was in the shop, and she had decided a brisk walk home at the end of her day would do wonders for her spirits. The route was very well lit, and she had walked it many times before. Her walk home was unnerving. She felt like someone was following her. The walk from her office to her cottage normally took thirty minutes at a comfortable walking pace. She was breathing heavily as she walked at a much quicker pace, sensing someone was close behind her. She clutched her keys in a defensive hold: keys protruding outward between her knuckles with the bulk of her keys inside her fist. Her dad had taught her to use this as a defensive approach to her car or under any circumstances when she was alone.

Paige breathed a slight sigh of relief as she approached her condo. She quickly entered and relocked the door. The security system had not been triggered, so she was confident that no one had been in her house. She was about to reset the security system when it occurred to her that if she did not, the system would make and automatic call to the police department to follow up on the alarm. By now, her heart was racing with panic. Her place was less than a thousand square feet. She went through the cottage to check all windows and doors. Paige's cell phone vibrated in her pocket. She looked at the missed call. A temporary wave of peace washed over her. The message was from Garrett. She listened to the message: "Paige, I love you and miss you." The great urgency in his voice worried Paige. "Paige, I have hired a detective (John) to provide 24/7 protection for you until we get through an investigation on the accident. We have uncovered some very unnerving information about Sam, and he may very well attempt to contact you. Call me as soon as you get this message. I love you."

Just as Paige hung up her phone, she was startled by an incoming call on her house line. It was the security system calling to verify the tripped alarm. She identified herself. She also requested that the police make a drive by to check on clues related to Paige's disappearance. The dispatcher explained that a lieutenant Walker was on the premises and would be coming to the door. "Ms. O'Connor, Lt. Walker needs to ask you some questions. I will stay on the phone with you until he is with you."

"Thank you. I think he may be here. There is a man at the front door."

"Ms. O'Connor, my name is John Walker. I am the private detective that Garrett hired several weeks ago. My badge and picture ID are in your mail slot. Would it be possible to come in?"

Paige was unsure as to allow this man in. She verified the badge and ID. "Lt. Walker has identified himself, and I am going to let him in. Thank you for your help." Paige hung up the phone.

"We believe we have a lead. I believe the name Sam Peterson means something to you."

"Sam?" Paige said with fear rising in her voice.

"Ms. O'Connor, there has been an ongoing investigation of Sam Peterson over the past two years. His involvement in drug dealing, money laundering, and associated crimes over the past two years has made him one of our major criminals on international and national radar. We were very close to closing in on his operation in December. Then your family's accident happened. My condolences to you, for your terrible loss. As hard as this may be for you to accept, there is a connection between Sam and the accident that killed your family. Sam was beyond desperate for money. His trail led us to confirm that he had hired an auto repair shop to disconnect the brakes on your parent's car the day before their fatal accident. That was the cause of their accident. We believe that he was under the impression that he would be a recipient of at least half a million dollars from their estate."

The information that Paige was hearing was too much to process. Her head was spinning with the knowledge that Sam murdered her parents and sister. She was somewhat relieved to learn that there was an ongoing investigation to locate Sam.

"Ms. O'Conner, we will be providing surveillance coverage/protection for you during the ongoing investigation. If you have any questions or concerns, please do not hesitate to call.

"Thank you, Lt. Walker."

Between the security system in her home and 24/7 protection, Paige felt safe.

THE TRAP

"Ring, ring….." It was 1:00 a.m. on Sunday morning… who is calling me at this hour? "Hello."

A slight pause on the other end of the line, followed by hysterical crying.

"Erika, is that you? What is wrong?"

Erika was crying so hard, Paige could hardly understand what she was saying. She thought she heard her say that she just received terrible news about her twin brother. Paige knew that Erika and her brother, Mitch, were very close.

"Paige, can you come stay with me?"

"Yes, of course. I will put together a few items and be on my way. "

Through sobs and heavy breathing, Erika managed to say, "I am staying at the summer manor in Gatwick."

Paige felt a great obligation to go support her. Erika has been a great friend and support over the past few months to Paige.

As Paige approached the manor, it was pitch black. She thought, perhaps the power is out, after all it is raining and there is a fairly gusty wind. Paige knocked on the door, but Erika did not answer. The eeriness of the dark sent a shiver down her spine. "Oh come on, you are not five. " Paige opened the door and walked into the foyer. "Erika, are you in here?"

"I am in the den" Paige made her way to the den, where she found Erika by the fire, drinking some wine, The room had a faint glow from the few candles lit and the fire. Paige made her way to the couch and sat down by Erika. She took her hands into hers and held them. Looking at Erika's tear stained face she asked her what had happened.

Erika indicated that she had received a phone call that her brother was in an accident and did not survive. He was in the states for business. With the storm, she knew it was not possible to travel until later in the morning. "You were the first person who came to mind for me to call. I knew that you would understand. I don't just cry in front of anyone."

"Will you stay here with me tonight?"

"Yes, of course," Paige answered, her voice filled with compassion.

Erika offered Paige a glass of wine. "You are probably chilled, from the rain. This will warm you up."

"Thank you. I could use a good glass of wine."

"Paige, I will go get you a blanket and pillow from the linen closet." While Erika was out of the room, Paige became light headed. She laid her head back on the couch. She thought, "that is what I get for not eating dinner last night." A few minutes later Erika returned. Paige felt very odd, as though she was in a fog. She told Erika that she was not feeling well and thought she should lay down.

Erika gave her the pillow and covered her with the blanket. Paige felt herself slipping in and out of consciousness. She could not tell if Erika was still in the room. At one point she thought that she heard voices, a man and woman talking.

A few hours passed and she woke up. At first she was not sure where she was. She lay thinking and remembered that Erika had called her, crying. Paige looked around the room to see if Erika was there. The room was still fairly dark. The room looked different. The fireplace was in a different location; the furniture was different. Was she in a different location? How could that be? The curtains were drawn, so Paige could not determine if it was daytime. She reached in her pocket to pull out her phone, but it was not there. She wondered if she had left it in her car. She sat up on the couch, her head pounding. She thought, how much wine did I drink to have a headache? She went to the window to pull back the curtain, only to find boarded up windows. That was alarming.

She heard voices in the foyer. "Erika, are you there?"

The door to the room was closed, probably to keep the heat in the room (Paige recalled that the power was out when she arrived). She heard the handle turn and Erika walked into the room. Paige could see the shadow of another person behind her. Someone much taller than Erika, the silhouette of a man. Erika moved to the side and the man stepped into view. The blood in Paige's veins froze…. It was Sam.

Paige stared in disbelief. Fear and random thoughts raced through her mind. How on earth did he get here? How did he know where to find me? What does he want? What happened to the 24/7 surveillance Lt. Walker put in place?

Sam moved towards Paige. He stood over her…"my long lost sister…. I told you I would get what I wanted. I always get what I want. You and I have a long future ahead of us. You will give me what is rightfully mine and no one will stop me this time. Your knight in shining armor is not here to save you this time." Sam's eyes were hallow, void of life.

Paige looked at Erika, who was standing by the fireplace, with her back to Paige. "Erika, you did this? Why? I trusted you. How could you be involved with Sam?"

Erika whipped around, facing Paige. Her eyes were a fiery red, almost as if she were possessed. She hissed, "I am not your friend. I have been using you, getting to know you to set you up for this moment. I belong to Sam. I do what he wants, no matter the cost."

Paige had felt fear before, but this was a different level. She was not sure if Erika was high on drugs or if something demonic was going on. "Father God, You are my protector, my guide. I trust You. Please protect me, give me courage and strength to overcome what is before me."

"I belong to the most high God. In His name I trust; and in the name of Jesus I claim protection from you."

Sam was always squeamish whenever confronted with the gospel. He immediately took Erika's hand and they left the room. The door was locked from the outside. Paige's mind was racing. What did Sam want? Money; the house? How am I going to get out of here? How did Erika get mixed up with Sam? How on earth was I so easily fooled by her? It was all becoming clear to Paige. Erika's preoccupation with Paige's past. Her curiosity and "panic response" to Paige's travel plans to Colorado in December. That must have caused a kink in their plans.

Paige could hear them talking about their next steps. "How are we were going to move Paige and to what location? We have to move quickly. She is a creature of habit and it will not take long for her assistant to notice she is missing." She overheard Erika tell Sam that they needed to get rid of

Paige's car. She could hear Sam's voice. His voice was full of rage. Paige remembered his anger, especially when he was using drugs." Paige read the panic in their voices as a sign that their plans were not as well designed as perhaps they had thought they were. Things were starting to unravel.

Paige heard the front door slam and then it was quite. Sam and Erika drove off in Paige's car. They drove it to an area and pushed it off a mountain road. The car rolled several times and landed in a ravine. "It will be days before they find her car," Sam taunted.

Paige sat in the dark room, praying. She was trusting that Tara would realize something was wrong and contact Lt. Walker and Garrett. She knew that her structured life; attention to detail, discipline and scheduling would pay off for finding her. The one bad thing is that Sam & Erika have a day head start. Paige has been missing since Sunday morning and it will be Monday morning before they realize something is wrong. What about the 24/7 surveillance? Had something gone wrong with that protection? Paige glanced at the floor by her feet. She noticed an object under the couch. She reached under and felt the familiar shape of her iPhone. Hope flooded her thoughts. She had a small battery charge. How did they not find her phone? Perhaps in their panic over shortage of time, they forgot to look or search her for her phone. Paige made sure the GPS locator was turned on, (it had been in the off setting). She quickly sent a "help text" to Garrett.

At 9:00 a.m. Monday morning, Tara contacted the local authorities and Garrett. She was positive that something happened to Paige. Paige had not shown up to the office, did not answer her phone, and the most disconcerting was when Tara stopped by her condo. It was evident that Paige had left in a hurry. Tara was familiar with Paige's daily routine. She contacted the athletic club where Paige worked out regularly. Paige had not been in. Paige's security system at her condo showed that she reset the security alarms at 2:05 a.m. on Sunday morning. There were no other activations to the system after 2:05 a.m. on Sunday. The setting was done remotely from her iPhone. That was enough information for Garret and Tara to be concerned about Paige's where-abouts. There was also the question about the surveillance. What happened to the individual on duty Sunday morning?

The investigator, Lt. John Walker asked about Paige's clients. Tara indicated that Paige had been working exclusively with one client over the past several months; Erika VanHieden. Lt. Walker indicated that he would have his office run a background on Ms. VanHieden. He also pulled her cell phone records and noted an incoming call at 2:00 a.m. from Ms. VanHieden. His background search pulled up Erika's records of attending a drug rehab center in the states, three years ago. She was a patient at the same time Sam Peterson was admitted. That was the connection.

It was clear that Paige was in danger. Her relationship with Erika over the past several months was based on trust from Paige's side of the relationship, but deceit and betrayal from Erika. She had set Paige up. The picture that Paige may have been kidnapped was becoming clear.

The VanHeiden family owned numerous properties throughout Europe. Determining which property was the possible location for Paige's abduction would be difficult. Based on Sam's history of violence and ability to hide, would add to the complexity of locating Paige.

The immediate search would focus on properties within a ten hour perimeter. Garrett was on a plane to London. The flight was the longest 7 hours of his life. As he was departing the plane his phone vibrated with a text. He was shocked to see it was from Paige. "GPS is on…. Find me….. low battery." Garret quickly linked his iPhone app to locate her phone to determine her location. Within seconds he had the location. He decided to start the drive to the location, before contacting Lt. Walker. Garrett was determined to be the person to put an end to Sam Peterson's interference in Paige's life. When he was within a few miles of the house he contacted Lt. Walker. "John, I received a text from Paige, communicating that her GPS signal was turned on. I am approximately two miles from the VanHeiden property. I have sent you a text with the address."

"Garrett, don't do something you will regret. I advise you to wait for local authorities and back up prior to accessing the house."

Garrett agreed to park his vehicle out of site and wait for the authorities. He parked in an area where he had full view of the front of the house. In the event Sam attempted to move Paige, he would be ready to intervene. Lt. Walker notified Garrett when the team was within a few minutes of arrival. The team was setting up a perimeter within 25 yards of the house and a secondary perimeter at 100 yards around the house. There would be no escaping for Mr. Peterson or Ms. VanHieden.

It was dusk; Garrett could see the swat team moving into position. He moved to the area where Lt. Walker was located. Several swat team members entered the house. It was several minutes before they came out the front door. The first person they escorted out was Ms. VanHieden. Several minutes passed before an officer came over the radio. "The house is clear. There is no sign of Peterson or Ms. O'Conner."

"Unbelievable!" Garrett shouted. "What is going on?" He got into Lt. Walker's face. "If your man assigned to surveillance for Paige had done his job, we would not be in this mess."

"Garrett, we are wasting precious minutes arguing over the mistakes made. We need to refocus on how they exited the…." Another officer came over the radio, "Lt. Walker, there is evidence of underground passage ways, accessible through the cellar. There is a team of 8 swat team members entering the passage way. It is a complex maze of tunnels. We will make our way through the tunnels to the exits."

Underground passage tunnels were a standard part of architectural design for homes in the World War II era. That was the time period this particular manor had been built. As soon as the officer identified there were underground passage ways, Garret pulled up archive drawings of the estate on his iPhone. He was able to pull a full drawing of the underground tunnels through an architectural library resource. The officer was right; the maze was a complex web of tunnels with multiple switch back turns and dead ends. The focus needed to be on exits. He worked with Lt. Walker to pinpoint the location of exterior exits from the tunnels. The swat team would need to move quickly to cover the tunnel exits before Sam and Paige reached one. The largest risk factor they were dealing with was time; how much of a head start did they have. Two of the exits were approximately a mile from the house. "all units advise when you are in position at your designated exit."

It seemed as though hours had passed by the time all teams radioed confirmation of their location to Lt. Walker. All teams reported, "Tunnel exits" are covered. The actual time that had lapsed was twenty was ten minutes. Lt. Walker's command: "All units armed, on standby; Peterson is armed, agitated and very dangerous."

In addition to the swat units posted at the tunnel exits, several officers were making their way through the maze of tunnels, toward the exits, to flush out Peterson and Paige. After an hour all tunnels had been swept. There was no sign of Sam or Paige. There was no evidence that anyone had exited the tunnels prior to the swat teams securing the exits. It was as if Sam and Paige had disappeared into thin air.

Garrett heard the roll call of all swat units, indicating the tunnels were clear and no activity at the exits. The team leader ended the radio communication with, "Lt. Walker, we await your directive."

"All units maintain position until further instructions."

SECRET PASSAGEWAY

G arrett was kneeling, with his head in his hands. "How could I be this close to Paige and fail to rescue her?" He stood up and made his way to the front door. He wanted to be where Paige was last. He walked into the room off the foyer. There was a slight residue of Paige's perfume in the air. She had to have been in this room. He sat on the couch; grasping the pillow in his hands he raised it to his face. The pillow was covered in her scent. His thoughts were interrupted by Lt. Walker. "Garrett, the teams have doubled back through the tunnels. Our best conclusion is that Sam and Paige made it to one of the furthest exits before the swat units were able to secure the exits. There is an all-points bulletin out across London for Peterson and

O'Conner. We will find them. There will be a full unit set here in the event they double back to get a vehicle."

Garrett was numb. Walker's words provided no comfort. Garrett was not about to give up. He and Paige belonged together. He stayed at the VanHieden property for the night. He wandered the halls of the manor, checking rooms, closets, storage areas. Hoping for a space the swat team missed. The library was the last room he entered. Old houses from this era often had a movable wall into another room. Garrett worked his way around the room looking for doors or a loose panel. To his amazement he found a wall that moved. Behind the wall was a staircase. Garrett descended into a room. The room had access to a single tunnel. Fear gripped Garrett. Was this tunnel separate from the maze of tunnels the swat team had searched? Had this tunnel provided a undetected escape route for Sam and Paige? Garrett made his way through the tunnel to find the exit. Just before he reached the exit he kicked something on the floor. Using the flashlight app on his phone, he looked at the floor. It was a cell phone, Paige's cell phone. The battery was completely out. That is why the GPS had not provided additional locator information once they arrived at the manor. Garrett exited the tunnel. He looked around to gauge his location. He was approximately a ½ mile south of the manor. He knew the road was close. He continued through the woods to the road. When he reached the road he called Lt. Walker.

"John, I found another exit route out of the house. I was wandering through the house and in the library, I came across a panel door that lead to a staircase. The stairs descended at least one story below the main floor into a small room. A single tunnel passage off that room, lead to an external exit. We missed this tunnel, as it was not noted on the original drawings. The tunnel exits a ½ mile below the house just above the main road. I found Paige's cell phone on the floor of the tunnel just before the exit. We know the direction we came. The best assumption is to conclude they have a several hour head start."

Garrett, I will communicate with our team."

Lt. Walker picked up Garrett and headed back towards Paige's condo. He wanted to look for anything that may give them a lead as to where Sam may take Paige. As they approached her driveway, Garrett noticed a rental vehicle in her driveway. Both he and Lt. Walker were alarmed. They drove past the driveway to park in an area where they would not be noticed. Walker radioed swat units to transport to their location; proceed with caution.

Garrett obtained security access time from Paige's security company. The code had been deactivated fifteen minutes ago. Garrett's heart raced, with the thought that Sam and Paige could be just a few feet away.

Swat arrived and surrounded Paige's condo. There was evidence of movement inside. Garrett could see the silhouette of a man through the front window. It had to be Sam. It took everything in him to not storm the door and strangle him with his bare hands. Swat confirmed that Sam was armed with a hand gun. The decision was made to wait them out. It was highly probable that they had stopped at Paige's to pick up some basic supplies, cash and her passport.

About 3:00 a.m. the front door opened slowly. Sam escorted Paige out the front door. Lt. Walker radioed his team to "hold your positions. Peterson has Ms. O'Conner at gun point." Sam and Paige drove off in the rental car. During the night, Garrett had checked activity on Paige's credit card. Two airline tickets were purchased; London to Scotland. Departure was in three hours. Lt. Walker contacted authorities to intercept Sam and Paige at the airport. That would be the safest location to minimize and injury. Sam would not make it past security with his gun.

John dropped Garrett at the main entrance where he met up with two undercover officers. They made their way to the boarding area. Garrett's heart was pounding as he walked briskly through the airport. Running would draw attention that he did not need or want. He arrived at the boarding gate and from a quick scan of the waiting area he was confident that he had arrived before Paige and Sam.

Garrett went to the coffee shop in the waiting area. He asked the cashier to do him a favor. Paige would not travel without a cup of coffee. He wrote a note inside a cup sleeve. He gave the sleeve to the cashier and asked her to use it specifically for a woman who would be getting a Venti Low Fat Vanilla latte. He showed the cashier a picture of Paige. He indicated that he was there as a surprise, so the cashier needed to be discreet. He also asked her to compliment Paige on her clothing. Something like, that sweater brings out your eyes. The thanked her and went to sit in an area where he had a 180 degree view of the waiting area.

Garrett anxiously waited, watching the traffic flow of people, looking for Paige; his heart pumping wildly in his chest. He had been waiting for about 10 minutes when he spotted them in the crowd. As predicted, Paige went to the coffee shop to get her latte. The cashier complimented her on her sweater. Paige paused for a moment, thinking "that is something Garrett would say." The cashier was about to hand Paige her coffee when she said, this is really hot, let me get you a sleeve protector. "Here is your change; I believe that you will have a very good day." The cashier's comment and smile made Paige wonder. Sam had waited for Paige at the entrance of the coffee shop. Sam and Paige made their way to two empty seats in the waiting area to wait for the plane. They would board in an hour. Garrett knew that waiting an hour would be difficult for Sam. As Paige sat down, the cup sleeve fell on the floor. As she picked it up she noticed writing on the inside of the sleeve. She immediately recognized the handwriting as Garrett's. It felt as if her heart was in her throat. She swallowed hard and took a deep breath as she quickly read the note. "I am here;

you are safe; trust me." She did not want to draw attention by looking around for Garrett. She slid the sleeve back on the cup. The next hour passed by painfully slow. Garret had a perfect view of Paige; however she could not see him. The plan was to allow them to board. They would be in the pre-boarding group, as they were traveling first class.

The boarding staff had already notified all first class travelers to delay their boarding. One exception was that two undercover officers would be boarding as first class travelers, seated behind Paige and Sam.

The overhead public address system clicked on. "Flight 2578 to Scotland is now boarding. Passengers seated in the first class cabin are invited to board at this time." Paige and Sam stood up and made their way to the boarding tunnel. Garret could sense Paige's apprehension and nervousness. He knew she was scared.

As Sam handed the attendant his boarding pass, Paige glanced around the waiting area hoping to catch a glimpse of Garrett. She was fairly certain that she saw him on the other side of a pillar. She had to trust that he was there and would step in at the right time. Sam turned to Paige and took her coffee cup from her. Her heart raced. "Thanks for saving me a sip." He snapped sarcastically as he threw the cup in the garbage.

Paige approached her seat, only to find it occupied. She looked at her boarding pass and then at the man in her seat.

"Excuse me sir, I think there is a mix up. You are in my seat. She showed him her boarding pass."

"You are so correct. My apologies." His traveling partner looked at his boarding pass and noticed that he too was in the wrong seat. "We are one row back. We'll grab our bags and move." Paige stepped behind their row, leaving a space in the isle for the men to move into in order to get to their correct seats. She could tell that both men were at least 6'4" tall. They both resembled Garret's build and she wanted to allow them enough space to move into their seats. The next few minutes were a whirlwind of action. Before she knew what was happening, the two men had Sam turned around, pinned to a seat and in handcuffs. Both men showed their law enforcement badges.

"Mr. Peterson, you are under arrest for the kidnapping of Ms. O'Conner, three counts of murder, multiple counts of possession and the intent to distribute narcotics, drug trafficking and money laundering." Sam was spewing profanity at the officers. He also threatened that he would be back and he would take care of his unfinished business with Paige. Paige heard one of the officers tell Sam, "Where you are going, you will never see the light of day." Both officers escorted Sam off the plane.

The pilot slipped into the first class cabin. "Ms O'Conner, please take a seat. There will be someone coming to escort you off the plane."

Back in the boarding area, as soon as Sam was out of the tunnel, Garret was cleared to board the plane to get Paige. He ran down tunnel to the door of the plane. He took two long strides to Paige's seat, scooped her into his arms and buried his face in her hair. They both were shaking from the myriad of emotions. He escorted her off the plane. Lt. Walker and a swat unit met them in the boarding area to accompany them out of the airport.

Although today's event marked a turning point in their lives, neither Garrett nor Paige would feel confident that this nightmare was completely over until Sam was behind bars. Based on Sam's criminal history, and the additional sentencing of three murders, he would be sentenced to life in prison without parole, possibly even the death sentence.

Garrett remained in London with Paige until Sam's sentencing was complete. He was not about to leave her side.

In late November Garrett returned to New York for a few weeks. He was planning to join Paige in Colorado for the holidays. During that time Paige was closing down her business in London. She was planning to relocate to Colorado and start a new journey.

CLOSURE

Paige's thoughts returned to the present. She felt as if she had just been awakened from a nightmare. In a sense, she had. The memories were sometimes so strong. It was as if during the past two hours, she had just relived the whole Christmas from *two years* earlier and every event that followed. She glanced out the window. By her calculations, she should be near the turn to her parents' house. Normally, she would be able to tell by familiar landmarks. But it was snowing heavily, and it was hard enough just to see the road in front of her. As she rounded the corner, the house was in sight. She was startled at the sight of lights on and smoke from the chimney. As she pulled in front of the garage, her headlights flashed across the front porch. There was Max, Uncle Paul, and Aunt Mary's German shepherd. Paige realized that Paul must be inside doing a routine check. *But, why a fire in the fireplace?* The garage door opened, and Paul was standing inside ready to greet Paige.

"Hi, princess," Paul said as he gave Paige a hug. Paige felt Max's head rubbing on the back of her leg. Paul and Paige walked into the house. It was obvious that Paul was expecting her arrival. He had a roaring fire going and hot chocolate ready. "Did you receive some inside information from Tara?" Paige asked with a wink. Paul just rolled his eyes. Again, Paige made a mental note to thank Tara. Although no one would ever replace Brittnae, God had already filled tremendous voids in her heart with the love, connection, and support she had from Tara, Paul, Mary, and Garrett.

"Mary should be arriving any minute with supper. We knew you would be tired after your long flight and drive. A little company and some warm food will do you some good. I will take your bags up to your room."

Paige was warming herself by the fire when she heard Mary at the front door. "Hi, sweetie. We have homemade turkey soup with your favorite bread. Two of your favorites, I believe. Give me a hug." Then Paige followed Mary into the kitchen.

"You look wonderful. How are you really doing?" Mary asked with the look in her eyes that said "It is me you are talking to. We have always been open and honest with each other."

"I am making progress, slowly but surely. You may have already heard the events that occurred leading to Sam's arrest. I believe he has made international news. The events of last week lead up to this trip. I needed to come back and say good bye to Mom, Dad, and Brittnae. As painful as it is, I need to close the door on the awful part of that Christmas two years ago. Until I close that door, I can't walk through the door of beauty that Garrett and I found. Sometimes, I think I could not go another minute let alone another day."

"Paige, honey, people heal in various ways and time frames. The pain of losing your family will never completely go away. From what you have shared with me, you are ready to put closure on the past and move on to pursue the rest of your life. I know one young man who is going to jump for joy when you do close that door."

"You know, young lady, that man's love for you is very deep." Mary and Paige looked up as Paul was standing by the banister, overlooking the family room. "You are blessed to have someone who cherishes and loves you the way he does."

Paige knew that Paul was right. She wanted to finalize things so she could go to Garrett.

"Paige, Sam was a very sick man. His addiction to cocaine and enormous gambling debts made him a walking time bomb. We are grateful for Garrett's insight and action to bring this to closure."

"On Garrett's last visit in early November, I made my decision to come home this Christmas for closure," Paige said.

"What is that beeping noise? Paul asked.

"Sounds like I have a fax. Would you excuse me for a moment?" Paige dashed to her office and saw a 911 alert from Tara: "CALL ME ASAP, I have not been able to locate Garrett."

When she returned to the family room, Paul and Mary had their coats on. "Is everything all right? You seem a little shaken."

"Everything is fine," Paige answered doing her best to keep from meeting Mary's eyes. Mary could read her better than her own mom ever could. "Tara is working out some details for a meeting I have while I am here in the states. She has run into a few kinks."

"We will give you the rest of your evening. Breakfast is at eight if you would like to join us."

Paige thanked them for dinner, hugged them, and watched them walk through the snow toward their house. Paul and Mary had been there for her so many times in her life. They were her family.

THE RANCH

Around the first year anniversary of the accident, Garrett had flown to Denver and drove straight to Paul and Mary's home.

"Garrett, what a pleasant surprise! Please come in," Mary greeted him so warmly. He felt so at home with them. They had been a haven for him.

"Come join us for some coffee and muffins," Paul said.

"I would be a fool to pass up Mary's cooking. I will get right to the purpose of my trip. I have taken a several-month sabbatical. I will stay in touch with my clients via technology. I am planning to be at the ranch, finishing the renovation. That is where I will finish my waiting period." Garrett saw the look of surprise on their faces.

"Does this mean that Paige is coming back?" Paul asked.

"From our last visit, I would say it is safe to say she will be here before Christmas. I know she will be here. The main reason I stopped by was to discuss something very important with you."

Garrett's last trip to London had given him tremendous hope that he and Paige would soon be together for good—perhaps, as soon as Christmas. Upon his return to the corporate office in New York, he had decided to take a short sabbatical from the office. His company had been operating very successfully for several years. His presence was not required on-site in everyday operations. With today's technology and a monthly, two-day business trip to each office location, Garrett enjoyed the benefits of a flexible work schedule. The balance of his time had been spent traveling to London to be with Paige and traveling to Colorado to renovate the house he purchased.

After Paige had lost her family, he knew it would take some time for her to work through her grief. He never dreamed it would take two years. After the first year, he decided to look into purchasing some property near Paige's parent's home. He knew that she would need to return there for closure. When she reached that point, he knew she would be free to love him and accept his love, and he wanted to be near.

A FAMILIAR MAP

Paige's thoughts shifted quickly to the fax she was holding. She called Tara. "Thank you for the alert message. Where could he be? For now, keep trying his office in New York. I will do some checking from here and update you on what I find. Thank you, Tara."

As Paige hung up the phone, her mind began to race, trying to figure where Garrett would be. She tossed and turned all night. Her sleep was filled with dreams as though the past two years were on video. She awoke to the soft chirping of birds. From her bed, she could see the fresh layer of snow that had fallen in the night. She slipped out of bed and pulled on her sweats, running shoes, hat, and gloves. A short run on a crisp, clear morning would be a great way to start the day. It had been years since she had

GINA BULLIS

run the road through the woods. As she ran, her thoughts went to Garrett. *I know I will find him.* She felt completely rejuvenated at the end of her run. As she approached the house, she could hear the phone ringing. She dashed up the steps and picked up the receiver.

It was Tara. "I have contacted his office. His secretary indicated that his location was to be revealed only to you." After disconnecting with Tara, she quickly dialed Garret's office. The phone rang for what seemed like eternity. Finally, a sweet voice answered, "Garrett Enterprises".

"Hello, this is Paige O'Connor, may I please speak with Bobbie?" Paige asked, her voice filled with anticipation.

"Hello, Paige. I have been expecting your call.

"Are you aware that I am trying to locate Garrett? Can you help me?"

"Yes, I have a map I will fax over to you."

"Thank you, Bobbie."

As Paige hung up the phone, a flicker of curiosity, anticipation arose as she considered receiving a map.

Bobbie hung up the phone. She immediately speed dialed Garrett in Colorado. "Garrett, I am faxing the map to Paige right now. Good luck. Don't worry about anything here. I will keep you posted to the important issues.

Garrett's heart swelled with excitement. As he hung up the phone, he closed his eyes and said, "Soon, I will have Paige in my arms—to stay. Thank you, Father."

Paige checked her fax machine. "Where is the fax?" She checked the ink cartridge, the paper. "What is taking so long?" The receive light lit up; Paige's heart skipped a beat. Paige was bewildered when she started studying the map. There was no indication as to what city or state was represented. She turned the map so she could read the names of the roads. She recognized every one of them. *Is he here? Could it be that Garrett is here, only minutes away? How could he be so close without me sensing his presence?*

Paige's eyes followed the directions to Garrett's location. She knew the place well. It was the horse ranch where they had gone horseback riding many times in high school. Her heart started pounding wildly like it had the night two years ago when she anticipated hearing Garrett express his feelings for her. Her mind kept racing from one thought to another as she showered. She put on a pair of black stretch pants and a beautiful, green sweater. She grabbed her coat, scarf, mittens, and headed out the door. She stopped briefly to pick up a box. It had some things she was taking to the gravesite. She had originally planned to take care of the gravesite visit before seeing Garrett. But her yearning to see him was too strong. It was as though the love she had for him was pushing past her pain. She had a sense of peace and joy that had been missing the past few years. For the past two years, her pain had been first. It was time to put her heart and love for Garret first.

As she drove, she was thinking of what to say to him. She had caused him so much pain, yet he waited for her. The house was less than a quarter mile away. Paige could see that someone was standing in front of the garage. She knew it was Garrett. She stopped the car and got out. Garrett was walking towards her. Paige ran to him and fell into his embrace. He buried his face into her hair and neck. He did not say anything. He just held her. After a few moments, Paige pulled away, only far enough for her to look at his face. She looked into his eyes, searching for his soul. "Garrett," she said, "I love you, and I am here to stay."

He bent down and kissed her with all the longing and passion he had been holding back. Paige's body melted into his. She wanted to give so much more. At the right time, she would. They turned and walked toward the house. As they entered the front door, Paige came to an abrupt stop. Garrett had completely recreated the cabin setting from the night two years ago. Taking her hands in his, he led her to the couch. There he knelt down on one knee and said, "I was going to ask you a question that night. I have waited two of the longest years of my life to ask you a question… Will you marry me?"

"Yes. Yes." she answered.

He moved to the couch next to her. As they sat down side by side, he pulled out a tiny, black box. Inside was the most exquisite diamond and sapphire ring Paige had ever seen. "Paige," he said, "there is more that I need to tell you.

I do not intend to let one more day go by without you by my side, as my wife. After Christmas, you can plan the kind of wedding you want. For now, I have made some arrangements for a simple ceremony to be performed this evening in the sunroom. I hope you will understand why I have done this. I have waited for so very long for the woman I love, and I do not want to wait any longer." Garrett's words were tender and full of desire. With a smile on her face, Paige answered, "I have waited fourteen years for the man I love. I do understand, and I would not have it any other way."

"Since it is our wedding," she said. "can you let me in on a few of the details?" Garrett was moved by the sparkle in Paige's eyes, the excitement in her voice. This was the Paige he knew and loved.

"Mary and I have taken care of all the details," he said, "She will fill you in."

Paige hesitated for a moment, and then she said, "There is something I need to take care of before the ceremony. Will you go with me to the gravesites?"

"Of course," he said. "I will go. I'll hitch up the team and sleigh and meet you out front in ten minutes."

SAYING GOOD-BYE

At the gravesite, Garrett followed Paige to the three headstones, carrying the box of evergreen bows and poinsettias. He set the box down by Paige then stood off to the side to give her some private time. Paige knelt down in front of the headstones and started talking. "Hello, Mum, Dad, and Brittnae. I know it has been a long time since I have been here. I have come to say good-bye to the painful memories of losing you. I miss you and always will. I have brought a very special person with me to share some news with you. I know you will remember Garrett Stevenson, Brittnae. You know how much I love him. Sis, he loves me too. We are having a simple ceremony tonight with Uncle Paul and Aunt Mary. I wish you were all here to celebrate with us. Daddy, you would approve of Garrett. He is a wonderful, caring gentleman who loves and treasures me more than I could have ever hoped for. He makes me very happy. Mum, I know that you approve of him. You always said he would make a fine husband."

The entire time Paige was talking, she was placing freshly cut evergreen boughs and poinsettias on their graves. Paige opened another box and started pulling out the pieces of the nativity scene that her dad had carved. As she placed each piece in the snow, she retold the Christmas story as her dad used to do every year. As she held the last piece in her hand, the carving of baby Jesus in the manger, she bowed her head. "Thank you for the gift of your son, and the new life he represents. Thank you for the gift you have given me, Garrett. Thank you for the new life we will begin today."

Garrett felt as though his heart would burst out of his chest. His love, pride, and admiration for Paige grew as he stood watching and listening. Paige lingered for a few more moments. She kissed each headstone. When she turned towards Garrett, their eyes locked. They had both waited so long for this day. Paige had an inner peace and joy that had been missing. She had closure. She was now free to love Garrett, completely.

Garrett pulled the sleigh into the barn. As he helped Paige down, he pulled her into his arms. His strength was exciting. She was very aware of the desire in his body.

"You have no idea how much I love you and want you," he said. "The next time I hold you, you will be my wife." His hands and eyes communicated more desire and yearning than his words.

Paige sweetly brushed his lips with hers. "I will meet you in the 'chapel' in two hours."

Garrett watched as Paige walked through the snow to the house. How blessed he was to have his woman. In two short hours, she would be his wife.

Paul greeted Paige at the back door. With a twinkle in his eyes, "Hey, princess, Mary is waiting for you upstairs."

A NEW BEGINNING

Paige's heart soared as she climbed the stairs. As she entered the room, she saw an elegant, white, Victorian-style wedding gown hanging on the front of the armoire across the room. As she walked closer, her eyes lit up. She recognized this dress. "Oh, Mary, it is more beautiful than I remembered."

"Paige, I always knew how much you loved my dress. I made up my mind several years ago that it would be yours on your wedding day. Let's see how it fits."

Paige was a little skeptical about how it would fit. Although Mary was a slender woman, Paige was smaller and a few inches taller. She gently stepped into the gown. She was astonished—it had fit perfectly. Paige turned to admire herself in the mirror. The beautiful lace sleeves ended in a V over the back of her hand. The lace bodice and drop waist fit like a satin glove. As Mary began the task of buttoning the multitude of pearl buttons that lined the back of the dress, Paige asked, "How did you manage this?"

"Well, I was a little frantic about this detail myself. Once Garrett had shared his plan to arrange the wedding, I knew I would need to have the gown altered to fit you. While talking with Tara about wedding details, she suggested shipping the dress to her. Since she is the same size, she had it tailored in London and sent it back with Garrett the last time he visited you. Now, here is your finishing touch." Mary handed Paige a beautiful headpiece made with fresh ivy and white and pink roses. Paige placed it on her head. "You are a vision, my dear." Paige was floating. She felt as if she had stepped into a fairytale. Everything was so perfect. Silently, she prayed, "Lord, thank you. Please protect this day."

"Now I had better get dressed." Mary opened the armoire and pulled out a beautiful Tea length, satin dress. Mary looked beautiful in the dress, delicately accented by a string of pearls. Paige looked at her in shock. "This is amazing. That dress is exactly what I had in mind for a bridesmaid dress. How could you know all the details of my dream wedding?"

"You will find out soon enough. Let's go see the chapel."

Mary led Paige to the sunroom of the back of the house. Once again, Paige was stunned at what she saw. It was as if she had entered her own dream. There was a white linen floor runner down the steps across the entire room and beautiful flower arrangements lining both sides of the isle. White and pink roses were arranged on a backdrop of ivy.

Mary handed Paige an envelope and said, "I need to attend to a few details in the kitchen." Paige stood in the middle of the sunroom. Everything was so incredibly beautiful. How could every detail of the wedding of her dreams have been planned by someone else? Paige glanced at the envelope in her hand. She recognized the handwriting. It was from Tara. The enclosed note read,

> *Paige,*
>
> *I hope everything turned out just as if you had done the planning. Actually, you did do the planning. I took very good notes, as you shared your dreams with me over the past several years. When Mary contacted me about Garrett's surprise wedding, she was thrilled when I shared your dream wedding down to the detail. She loves you as if you were her own daughter. I only wish I could be there to share your special day.*
>
> *Love, Tara*

There was a tiny object wrapped in delicate tissue paper inside the note. Paige unwrapped the tissue paper to find the ring that she had picked out for Garrett in London. On the inside of the ring, the inscription read, "My love to you, always and forever."

Mary touched Paige's shoulder just as she finished reading the note. Her eyes were filled with tears. "Oh, Paige, maybe we should have done your makeup last."

"No, no, I am all right. I will never be able to thank you, Paul and Tara for all you have done to make our wedding all that I dreamed it would be."

"Oh, honey, the guys are coming. We need to go into the other room."

Paige watched Garrett stride across the back walkway. He was so incredibly handsome—and he was all hers. Garrett walked to the front of the chapel—his gaze fixed on the opened French doors, anxiously awaiting Paige's entrance. Paul stopped as he entered the dining area where Paige and Mary were waiting. "You are both visions of beauty," he said, and then he tenderly kissed Mary on the cheek. He turned to Paige, holding her hands, eyes full of pride, brimming with tears, "We could not be more proud of you if you were our own daughter." Soft music was coming from the sunroom. Clearing his throat, he said, "There is an anxious young man waiting for you. Let's get this show on the road."

Mary elegantly drifted down the aisle. Paige watched Paul admire his bride. She thought about the beautiful testimony their marriage had been to her.

"It's your time, princess." Paul's voice interrupted Paige's thoughts.

The moment Paige entered the sunroom, her eyes locked onto Garrett's. She could feel the power of his love as she closed the distance between them. They stood a few moments lost in each other's gaze. The ceremony was simple. As Paige placed the ring on Garrett's finger, she looked into his eyes and said, "This ring represents my unending love for you that courses through my veins and is engraved on my heart, always and forever."